Raintree is an imprint of Capstone Global Library
Limited, a company incorporated in England and
Wales having its registered office at 264 Banbury
Road, Oxford, OX2 7DY – Registered company number:
6695582

www.raintree.co.uk
myorders@raintree.co.uk

Edited by Donald Lemke and Gena Chester
Designed by Hilary Wacholz
Production by Kathy McColley
Originated by Capstone Global Library Ltd
Printed and bound in India

ISBN 978 1 4747 6647 0
22 21 20 19 18
10 9 8 7 6 5 4 3 2 1

British Library Cataloguing in Publication Data
A full catalogue record for this book is available
from the British Library.

Batman created by Bob Kane with Bill Finger

BATMAN
TEENAGE MUTANT NINJA TURTLES
ADVENTURES

THE FACE OF TWO WORLDS

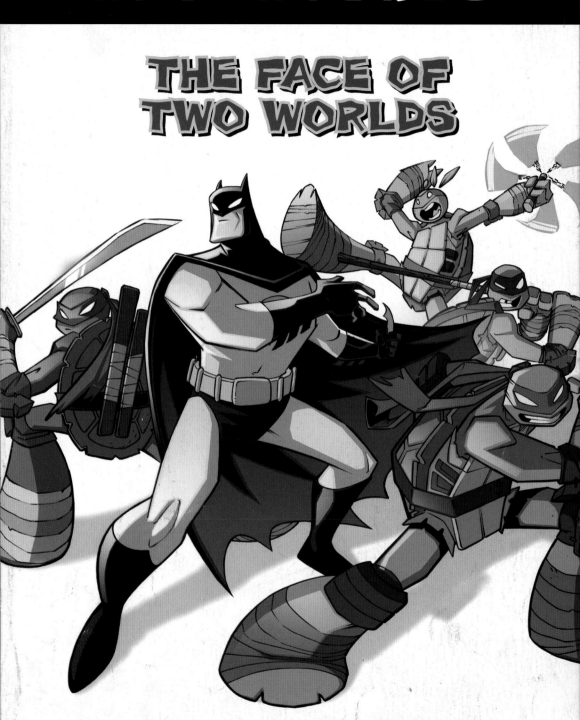

WRITER: **MATTHEW K. MANNING** | ARTIST: **JON SOMMARIVA**
INKER: **SEAN PARSONS** | COLOURIST: **LEONARDO ITO**

 raintree

a Capstone company — publishers for children

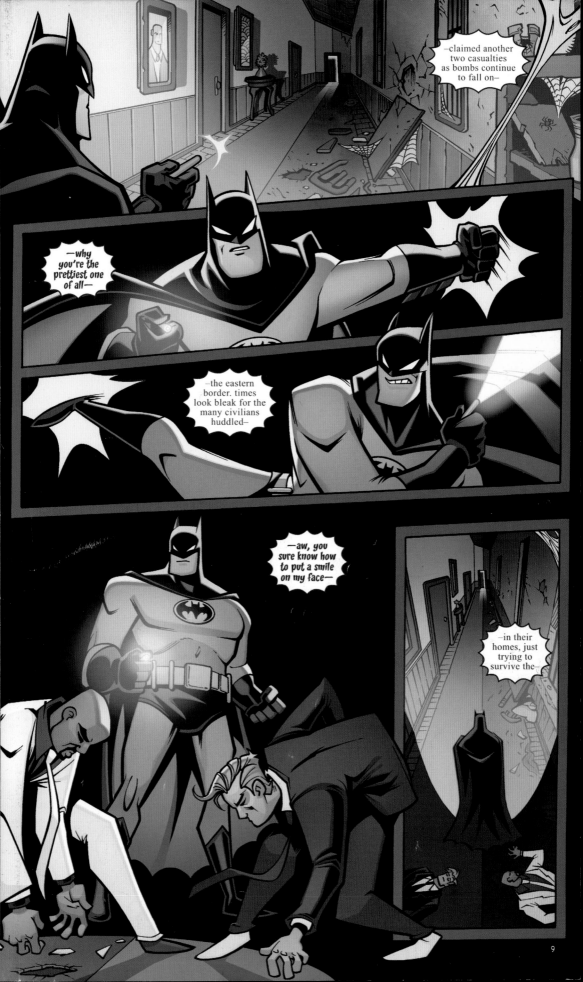

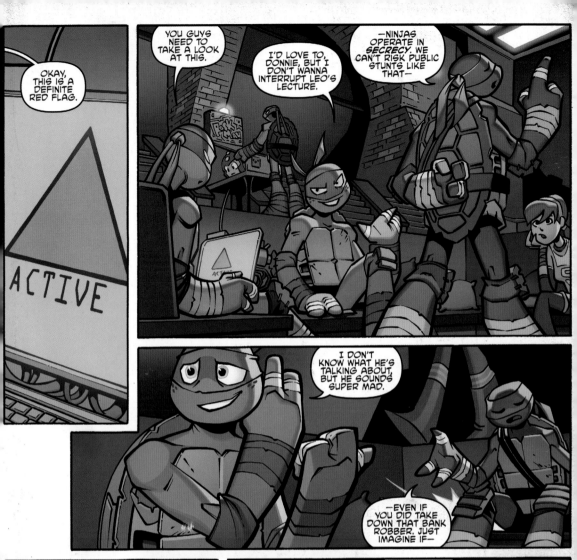

OKAY, THIS IS A DEFINITE RED FLAG.

ACTIVE

YOU GUYS NEED TO TAKE A LOOK AT THIS.

I'D LOVE TO, DONNIE, BUT I DON'T WANNA INTERRUPT LEO'S LECTURE.

—NINJAS OPERATE IN *SECRECY*. WE CAN'T RISK PUBLIC STUNTS LIKE THAT—

I DON'T KNOW WHAT HE'S TALKING ABOUT, BUT HE SOUNDS SUPER MAD.

—EVEN IF YOU DID TAKE DOWN THAT BANK ROBBER, JUST IMAGINE IF—

GUYS, I HATE TO BE THE VOICE OF REASON YET AGAIN, BUT YOU NEED TO STOP THE SQUABBLING AND CHECK THIS OUT.

LIKE, NOW.

APRIL O'NEIL.

The voice of reason. Like she said. Pay attention, already!

IS THAT WHAT I THINK IT IS? THEY'RE BACK?

YEAH. I THINK SO. THERE'S DEFINITELY BEEN PORTAL USE.

AND IT'S STILL ACTIVE.

IT'S *THE KRAANG*.

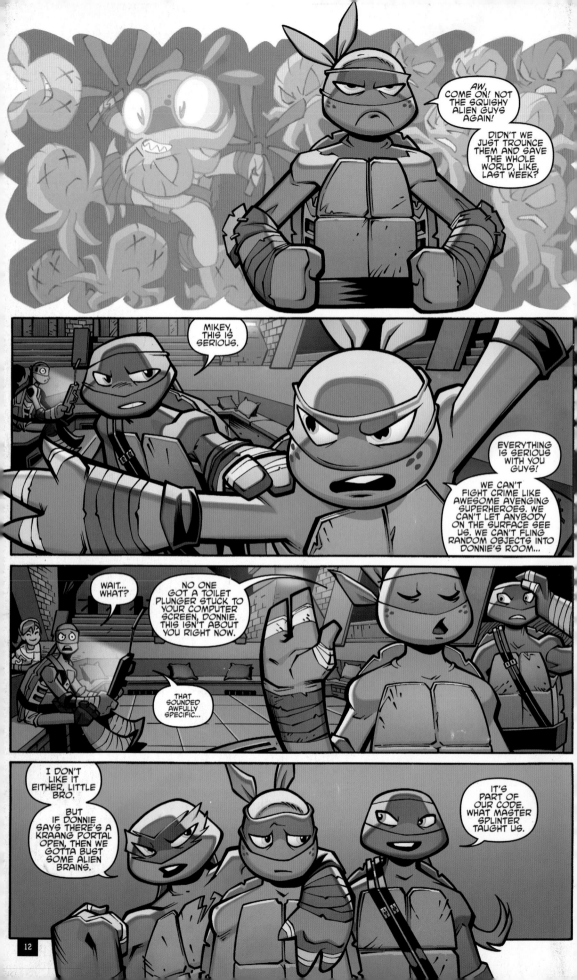

"WE GO WHERE WE'RE NEEDED."

TETCH, JERVIS

JOKER, THE

ENT HARVEY

HM.

—BACK NOW IN PROCESSING THANKS TO THE BAT.

SO HE'S THE ONLY ONE WHO'S BEEN RETURNED?

YEAH, SO FAR. STILL NO WAY OF KNOWING HOW HE GOT OUT, THOUGH. SECURITY CAMERAS WERE ALL FRIED, JUST LIKE WHEN THE OTHERS ESCAPED.

ISLEY, PAMELA

HUH.

WELL, LET'S GET THIS CELL READY.

PLACE IS A MESS.

CASH, A

CONGRATULATIONS, DONNIE.

YOU OFFICIALLY FOUND THE CREEPIEST CORNER OF THE NEW YORK CITY SEWER SYSTEM.

AND THAT'S EVEN COUNTING MIKEY'S ROOM.

SORRY, RAPH. THIS IS WHERE THE ENERGY TRAIL LEADS.

IF THERE REALLY IS AN OPEN KRAANG PORTAL, IT'S SOMEWHERE AROUND HERE.

GUYS!

THERE. THAT'S IT, RIGHT?

EVERYONE ON GUARD. IF SOMETHING CAME HERE THROUGH THAT PORTAL, IT'S NEARBY.

NOT RIGHT NOW, *ALFRED*. THANK YOU.

I'M SHOCKED, SIR. AND HERE I WENT AND PREPARED THIS GENEROUS PORTION OF NOTHING.

NOW IT WILL ALL GO TO WASTE.

ALFRED PENNYWORTH.

Batman's butler and right-hand man. Rarely shocked.

I DON'T SUPPOSE YOU COULD SPARE SOME TIME FOR A LATE-NIGHT DINNER, MASTER BRUCE?

CUTE, ALFRED.

SO WHAT'S THE CONUNDRUM OF THE EVENING, IF YOU DON'T MIND MY ASKING?

TWO-FACE. HE'S BACK IN ARKHAM NOW, BUT I CAN'T GET OVER THE WAY HE WAS RANTING EARLIER. ABOUT ANOTHER WORLD.

IT WAS INSANE. EVEN FOR HIM.

ARKHAM ESCAPPES:
> TWO-FACE - APPREHENDED
> THE JOKER
> HARLEY QUINN
> SCARECROW
> MAD HATTER
> CLAYFACE
> POISON IVY

AND THEN I FOUND THIS... ENERGY RESIDUE AT HIS OLD CELL. IT'S LIKE NOTHING FROM THIS PLANET.

I PROGRAMMED THE BATCOMPUTER TO LOCATE ANY SIMILAR SPIKES IN POWER. IF THERE ARE ANY OTHERS, WE SHOULD KNOW ABOUT THEM SHORT—

beep beep beep

ALFRED, CALL IN ROBIN ON THIS ONE. HAVE HIM MEET ME AT THE COORDINATES ON THE SCREEN.

WHATEVER THAT ENERGY IS...

22

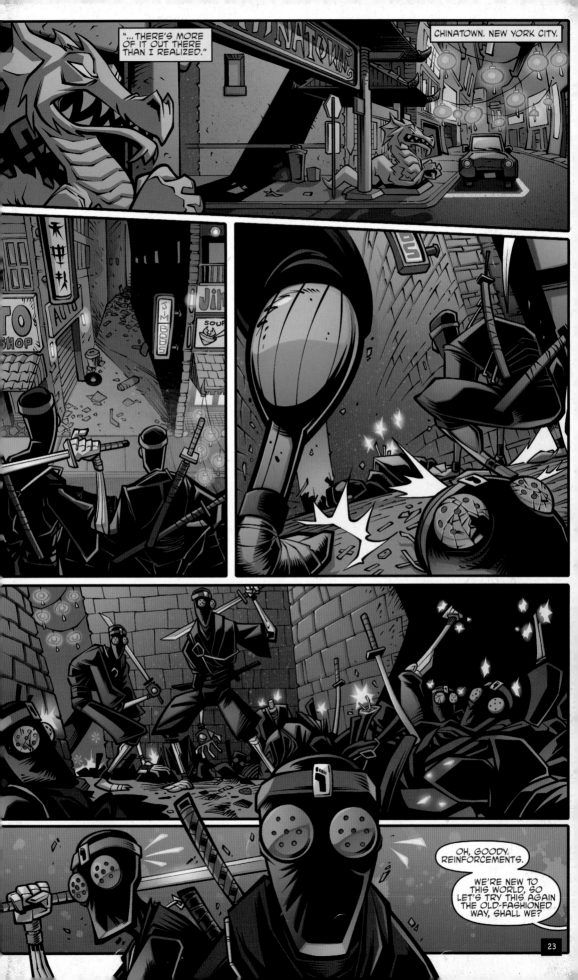

"...THERE'S MORE OF IT OUT THERE THAN I REALIZED."

CHINATOWN. NEW YORK CITY.

OH, GOODY. REINFORCEMENTS.

WE'RE NEW TO THIS WORLD, SO LET'S TRY THIS AGAIN THE OLD-FASHIONED WAY, SHALL WE?

CREATORS

MATTHEW K. MANNING

THE AUTHOR OF THE AMAZON BEST-SELLING *BATMAN: A VISUAL HISTORY*, MATTHEW K. MANNING HAS CONTRIBUTED TO MANY COMIC BOOKS, INCLUDING *BEWARE THE BATMAN*, *SPIDER-MAN UNLIMITED*, *PIRATES OF THE CARIBBEAN: SIX SEA SHANTIES*, *JUSTICE LEAGUE ADVENTURES*, *LOONEY TUNES* AND *SCOOBY-DOO, WHERE ARE YOU?* WHEN NOT WRITING COMICS, MANNING OFTEN WRITES BOOKS ABOUT COMICS, AS WELL AS A SERIES OF YOUNG READER BOOKS STARRING SUPERMAN, BATMAN AND THE FLASH. HE CURRENTLY LIVES IN NORTH CAROLINA, USA, WITH HIS WIFE, DOROTHY, AND THEIR TWO DAUGHTERS, LILLIAN AND GWENDOLYN.
VISIT HIM ONLINE AT WWW.MATTHEWKMANNING.COM.

JON SOMMARIVA

JON SOMMARIVA WAS BORN IN SYDNEY, AUSTRALIA. HE HAS BEEN DRAWING COMIC BOOKS SINCE 2002. HIS WORK CAN BE SEEN IN *GEMINI*, *REXODUS*, *TMNT ADVENTURES* AND *STAR WARS ADVENTURES*, AMONG OTHER COMICS. WHEN HE IS NOT DRAWING, HE ENJOYS WATCHING FILMS AND PLAYING WITH HIS SON, FELIX.

GLOSSARY

asylum hospital for people who are mentally ill and are unable to live without help

casualty person or thing injured, lost or destroyed

civilian person that is not in the armed services or police force

coordinates set of numbers used to show the position of something on a map

fertilizer substance added to soil to make crops grow better

generous larger than is usual or necessary

inmate prisoner

portal path between dimensions, worlds or realms

reinforcements extra troops sent into battle

residue what is left after something burns up or evaporates

secrecy being secret

security methods used to protect something

sewer system, often made up of underground pipes, that carries away liquid and solid waste

squabbling having a noisy argument

trounce defeat heavily, crush or overwhelm

unconscious not awake

vengeance paying someone back for personal harm

DISCUSSION QUESTIONS AND WRITING PROMPTS

1. HOW DO YOU KNOW THAT BATMAN AND THE NINJA TURTLES ARE INVESTIGATING THE SAME THING?

2. HOW CAN YOU TELL THAT THE TURTLE ON THE FAR RIGHT ISN'T MICHELANGELO?

3. IN THIS SCENE, BATMAN INVESTIGATES HOW TWO-FACE ESCAPED FROM HIS CELL IN ARKHAM ASYLUM. WRITE AND DRAW PANELS EXPLAINING HOW TWO-FACE DID IT.

4. WHAT DO YOU THINK HAPPENED TO CLAYFACE AFTER HE WAS PUSHED THROUGH THE PORTAL? WRITE A SCENE DESCRIBING WHERE HE GOES AND WHAT HE DOES NEXT.

READ THEM ALL!

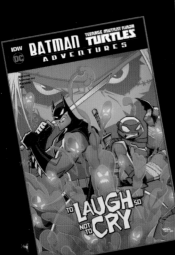

BATMAN TEENAGE MUTANT NINJA TURTLES
ADVENTURES